Moonlight Tales From A Far

Doris Oji

AuthorHouse™
1663 Liberty Drive
Bloomington, IN 47403
www.authorhouse.com
Phone: 1 (800) 839-8640

Because of the dynamic nature of the Internet, any web addresses or links contained in
this book may have changed since publication and may no longer be valid. The views
expressed in this work are solely those of the author and do not necessarily reflect the
views of the publisher, and the publisher hereby disclaims any responsibility for them.

Any people depicted in stock imagery provided by Getty Images are models,
and such images are being used for illustrative purposes only.
Certain stock imagery © Getty Images.

This book is printed on acid-free paper.

ISBN: 978-1-7283-5169-8 (sc)
ISBN: 978-1-7283-5170-4 (e)

Print information available on the last page.

Published by AuthorHouse 04/20/2020

authorHOUSE®

In loving memory of my late father,

Elder Emmanuel Oti,

who spearheaded girls' education in Arochukwu.

Acknowledgment

Grateful thanks to the following Aro men and women who retold these stories to me: Hon. Pius O. Nlewedim, Pastor James L. Kanu, Mazi David Ohabuiro, Rev. Mrs. Harriet Okereke, and Onyebuchi Obasi. Grateful thanks to my husband, Prince Joshua Kanu Oji (JP), and my children for their encouragement, Alessandro Ragazzi for his very useful comments, and my sister Nwanganga Shields for editorial comments.

Introduction

Before the advent of electricity, in many Arochukwu communities, families would gather outside the house of the compound chiefs on the nights of the full moon and tell stories to their children. The subjects of these stories are invariably fish, insects, or other animals with human-like qualities. These stories were used to impart life lessons to the children or to explain the world around them. The stories in this book have been passed from generation to generation, and my objective in writing these oral stories down is to preserve them for future generations.

1. Why Some Tortoises Live in the River

In the village of the Tortoise, Mr. Tortoise was looking for a wife. He had not found one that suited him among families of his acquaintance, so he set out in search of one. He travelled east until he came to a big expanse of water, sat on the shore, and admired the calm surface. The sun's rays reflected beautiful colors. He was enchanted and said to himself, "I wish I could find a wife as beautiful and as dazzling as this scene."

As he sat there, he heard a voice from the ocean, because he was indeed looking at the ocean.

"Are you looking to marry?" the ocean said.

He looked around until he found the spot the sun's rays pointed to. "Yes, if only I could find her. I have searched far and wide but have not found a girl as beautiful as this." He pointed to the spot.

"Well," replied the voice from the ocean, "look no further. I have just the right woman for you. Whenever the sun is shining, its rays will make her dazzle, and all the men in your village will be jealous of you."

Mr. Tortoise could not believe his ears. "Where is she? I want to see her immediately."

The voice from the ocean said, "One of my daughters lives in the east of your village. She has produced many daughters, and one of them is still unmarried. She is the most beautiful of them all. She is always calm, and her skin is smooth and translucent, allowing you to see her veins. She is called River. When you see her, you will love her."

And so it came about that Mr. Tortoise married River. He brought her back to his village, and there they lived. She was the most beautiful of all the wives in the village and the great love of his life. All his friends were happy for him and wished him a long marriage that would produce many beautiful children.

One day River decided to surprise Mr. Tortoise by preparing a special meal. Other Tortoise women had told her that akidi bean was much loved by the Tortoise clan, so she went to the market and bought a bushel of fresh akidi beans, and then she bought fresh fish and crayfish from her fellow river wives. That evening, she prepared a sumptuous feast served in her favorite pot. Then, having decked herself out in her finest wrapper and bubba, she sat in a spot where the sun's rays directly shone on her to eat. The aroma of the food filled the place.

Mr. Tortoise was just returning from afar. Dazzled by his wife's beauty and the aroma of the food, he rushed home. When he saw his wife busily eating, he sat down opposite her and said, "River, where is my portion?"

River looked at him with sorrowful eyes and said, "Sorry, I cooked only enough for myself. There is none left for you. But I am willing to share it if you could tell me the dish's name."

"What?" cried the Tortoise in disgust. "You must be joking! I do not know the name. Let me eat. I am hungry."

River shook her head. "I have told you, this food is only for me unless you tell me the dish's name."

Mr. Tortoise did not know what to do. "I can't believe this?" shouted Mr. Tortoise.

His raised voice attracted a crowd of his neighbors who taunted him and told him to beat his wife into submission. But he did not want a fight, so he quietly got up and went to the market. At the food stand, a food on sale resembled what he saw his wife eating. He sidled up to the stand and deliberately knocked over a pot of the food.

The stall keeper was furious. "You clumsy tortoise!" she shouted. "You have knocked over my akidi. What harm have I ever done to you?"

Having achieved his objective, Mr. Tortoise chanted, "Akidi akidi, kerede kerede." He continued this chant as he made his way home. Unaware of where he was going, he walked into a boulder on the road and knocked his leg. In his anguish and pain, he forgot what he had been chanting, so he ran back to the market, where he met a young boy who was selling ground nuts.

He went up to the boy and said, "Good fellow, may I sit next to you? I hurt my leg and the pain is too much to bear."

The boy said, "Oh, I am so sorry to see you in such pain. Sit here and rest a while."

After some time, Mr. Tortoise said to the boy, "Good fellow, tell me the name of the food that woman is selling. I have never seen it before."

The boy cast his eyes in the direction Mr. Tortoise was pointing and without hesitation said, "It is akidi. It is a very popular food here. It is delicious. You can see the crowd around the seller. Only very few women can make it. I can't believe you have never tasted it."

Having obtained the information, Mr. Tortoise stood up, rubbed his sore leg, and hobbled away.

At home, River was just putting away the leftover akidi so she could lie down to rest when her husband arrived. She looked up as he entered the room and greeted him warmly.

He looked at her lovingly and said, "Please give me some akidi to eat."

Surprised, his wife brought out the rest of the food out and invited the other tortoises in the village to partake in the sumptuous feast.

As they ate, Mr. Tortoise said, "Patience has its rewards."

After eating, the crowd swarmed into the river to swim. Some of them returned to shore, but others enjoyed themselves so much that they chose to live in the water and only came to shore to rest. Beginning that day, those tortoises that lived in the water have been called turtles.

2. Tit for Tat

It was a period of great shortage and famine in the village of the Tortoise clan. What the animals lacked most was salt. They could always find some food by scrounging among the withered vines and shrubs or in the brown grass, but salt was very hard to come by, and its lack cast a pall on the lives of the villagers. The village chief called a meeting to see how to solve the problem. At the meeting, it was decided that an emissary should search far and wide for salt. They knew that if someone went south, that tortoise would come to the ocean and would surely be able to bring back some salt, perhaps in the form of saltwater. Mr. Tortoise was chosen as the one to go.

After a very arduous journey during which he passed through mountains and hills and thick forests, he came upon a salt mine. He saw a big hole occupying many acres of land where big machines dug out salt from the earth and loaded it into big trucks, which then emptied the salt on a conveyor belt. At the end, the salt was bagged and transferred to other trucks that carried the bags to a warehouse for storage.

At the warehouse, Mr. Tortoise saw traders lining up to buy the salt, and he joined the line. When it was his turn, the man at the counter said, "How many bags do you want?"

"One!" replied Mr. Tortoise.

"Sorry, sir, this depot is for wholesalers only," the counter clerk said, and he then shouted, "Next!"

Undeterred, Mr. Tortoise said, "I only want one bag of salt. My people are desperate, and I have come from afar to this place. I will not leave without a bag of salt."

The counter clerk said angrily, "If you do not move out of the way, I will call police to remove you."

Mr. Tortoise stood his ground. An argument ensued, and the counter clerk called the police on his emergency phone. Then a trader interceded.

"Come, Mr. T," the trader said. "I will sell you one of my bags of salt. The counter clerk is only following the rules. Come with me."

He led Mr. Tortoise to his storage area, where the trader helped him tie a rope around a bag of salt and fasten one end to Mr. Tortoise's right hand. Satisfied, Mr. Tortoise proceeded to drag the bag of salt home.

On his way, he came upon Lizard City. Full of joy that he had accomplished his task and looking forward to being feted by the elders of his village, he continued his journey through the streets, admiring the beautiful flowers and intricate thatched roofs. He tipped his hat to several lizards lazing in the bright sunshine and some who were occasionally catching flies as they passed by. As he passed a particularly attractive house, he spied in front of him a lizard wench with sparkling iridescent scales. He stopped to flirt with her. As he turned the corner, he saw a group of male lizards loitering around. He waved at them and continued his journey.

Just then, one of the lizard bucks noticed what he thought was a bag of salt that appeared to be dragging itself. He detached himself from the crowd, ran to quickly cut the rope, and dragged the bag to his house. Satisfied, Mr. Lizard admired his find and then showed it off to his lizard neighbors.

When Mr. Tortoise realized that his bag was gone, he became upset and began a search. He went around asking if anyone had noticed someone with a bag. Luckily for him, one of the passersby directed him to a house not far from where he was. There he found it in Mr. Lizard's front yard, surrounded by many lizards.

"That is my bag of salt!" cried Mr. Turtle.

"Who said it is?" shouted Mr. Lizard. "I found it on the street. I did not see you holding it."

Dismayed, Mr. Tortoise went home and reported the incident to his elders, who convened a powwow to decide what to do. They determined that the councils of elders of the lizard and tortoise clans should meet to decide the matter.

When the day came, both sides presented their cases.

In his testimony, Mr. Tortoise said, "I was able to secure a bag of salt after an altercation with the counter clerk in the shop next to the salt mine. It was a big bag, and I knew that I could not carry it on my head, so I bought a big rope." He showed part of the rope to the assembly. "The retailer who sold me the salt bag helped me to tie one end of the rope around the bag and the other to my body so that I could drag the bag. Your Honor, I have a witness." The retailer then gave evidence to corroborate what Mr. Tortoise had said.

In his defense, Mr. Lizard said, "My elders, I can swear that the bag was lying on the road when I found it. I did not see anybody holding the other end of the rope. I saw Mr. Tortoise at the end of the street chatting with a woman, but he was nowhere near the salt." He then called many lizard neighbors as witnesses to confirm what he had said.

After a day's deliberation, the elders decided that Mr. Lizard did not steal the bag of salt and was wrongly accused. They chastised Mr. Tortoise for his carelessness.

Some days went by. Then, Mr. Lizard came to the tortoise village to buy some goods. As he was preparing to go home, it started raining just as he passed Mr. Tortoise's house. The rain was especially heavy, so Mr. Lizard knocked on the front door, but Mr. Tortoise was not home. Mr. Lizard then looked for a place where he could sit out the rain and found a small hole beside the front door. He squeezed in and waited for the rain to abate. Suddenly, he was struck with pain. He had lost his tail!

Apparently, Mr. Tortoise came home and saw a mysterious tail sticking out of the hole next to his door. Thinking it belonged to something that was a danger to him and his family, he ran into his house, brought out a sharp knife, and sliced the tail off. Mr. Lizard scrambled out, crying.

Shocked, Mr. Tortoise said, "I did not see you. I was not expecting you to be here."

That was how Mr. Tortoise paid Mr. Lizard back for the loss of the bag of salt.

3. The Fox and the Lion

It was night in the forest, and the animals were out in force to catch their prey. In the heat of the moment, a bear and a lion found themselves pursuing and then killing the same deer. They found the dead deer lying on the path. As it was not clear whether it was the same deer they were after, both claimed it and none would give in. A fight ensued. The animals tore at each other, and neither would allow the other to get near the spoil. Many other animals gathered to watch. Then, the jackal saw an opening, so he grabbed the deer and ran off, congratulating himself on his foresight, for the deer would make a nice feast for his clan.

The fighters spied him running away with the dead deer, stopped slugging each other, and ran after the jackal. Soon both were extremely tired and unable to pursue the jackal further. The lion said to the bear, "My dear friend, we have been very foolish. We could have shared our spoil if you had not been so greedy and selfish. Now what have you gained? That thieving jackal has made off with the deer."

The fight had sapped the old lion him of his strength, and he had none left for hunting for food. He lay on the side of a track for a while, unable to move, and then he dragged himself to his house, where he thought of nothing but food and how to get it. Then a thought came to his head when a field mouse trotted past. In his sweetest, most friendly voice, he called out to the field mouse, "Hi, my friend. Come over here. I will not harm you. I am dying."

At first the field mouse hesitated and moved as far away from the lion as he could to watch him from a safe distance. Satisfied that the Lion was telling the truth, he approached the lion again, sat down beside him, and comforted him, saying, "Mr. Lion, I am sorry to see you in such a plight. Is there anything I can do to alleviate your pain?"

The lion said, "Just being my friend is the best thing you can do for me. All my clan members have deserted me because I am dying and unable to provide for them. I will always cherish our friendship as long as I live."

The mouse felt sorry for the lion, so he asked again whether there was anything he could do for him.

Emboldened, the lion said, "Well, there is one thing you can do. You can spread the news of my impending death throughout the animal kingdom. I would really like a visit from all the animals so that I can tell them how sorry I am that I was not a good ruler."

The field mouse went out and spread the news and the lion's request for visits. Believing that the request was genuine, the animals sent emissaries to the lion, but each animal that approached was eaten by the cunning lion, and he was gradually getting his strength back. However, the fox refused the invitation.

On his return, the field mouse, not knowing what had occurred, told the lion about the fox's refusal.

"Oh, my best friend," said the Lion, "I really need the fox to come so that we can become friends. Please, go to him and implore him to come. I have to see him before I die."

So off trotted the field mouse to the fox's den to convince him to pay his respects to the dying lion. The fox finally agreed to come. First, he scouted the area where the lion lived, and then he approached the lion, stopping at a point where the lion could not reach him.

The lion said, "My very best friend, how kind of you to accept my invitation to visit me. You do not have to stand so far away. Come and sit down next to me so that we can resolve all our differences before I die."

"Thank you, Mr. Lion," said the fox, "but I think I am better off where I am. We can still talk, if you want."

"You see," said the lion, "I am too ill to shout, and I need you near me so that you can hear what I have to say. Why are you afraid to come near? I am too weak to harm you."

"Sorry, Mr. Lion, but I do not want to come near you. From where I am, I can see the tracks of your other visitors leading to your dwelling, but I have not seen any tracks leading outside. From this, I know that none of the animals who visited you came out alive. I do not want that to be my fate." The fox turned around and went home. That was how the fox outwitted the lion.

4. The Scorpion and the Turtle

In a big jungle where all the species of birds, insects, and other animals lived, there was a scorpion that was very difficult to deal with. It stung anything that came near it, whether or not they meant it any harm. It was just in his nature to sting anything that touched him. As a result, all the animals avoided playing with the scorpion or even coming near him. The result was that he had no friends in the forest.

Most evenings, the animals would gather at the jungle's watering hole to drink and socialize. The scorpion wanted very much to join them and perhaps get a ride across the water to the other side, where his scorpion family members had their nests and he was sure of making friends with other scorpions, thereby ending his loneliness. He also knew that if he crossed over, he would find abundant food since there were so few other animals there because of the prevalence of scorpions.

He sat on his perch staring sadly at all the animals and birds frolicking and laughing in the water He knew that if he were to approach them, the animals would all run away. He thought, *I must cross the water. I can no longer abide this loneliness.*

The scorpion could not swim, and if he tried to, he would drown. He saw several logs floating in the water, but they were too far for him to jump on from his perch. He thought and thought and thought until his head ached. Just when he though his head would break open because of all the thoughts passing through it, he saw a turtle get out of the water and look for a dry spot still warm from the last of the day's fast fading sunshine. At last, the turtle settled on a flat stone not too far from the blade of grass where the scorpion perched. Just as the turtle was about to recede into its shell, the scorpion called out, "Hello, my friend. You must be tired after all the commotion in the watering hole."

The turtle started and looked around to see who was talking to him but could not locate the individual. "I wonder who has the audacity to talk to me in this way. It cannot be someone I know." Without giving it any more thought, he settled down again to rest.

A minute passed and the scorpion said, "I am still here. You just did not think of looking up at the blade of grass behind you."

"Who are you?" said the turtle.

"I am your new friend, the scorpion."

When the turtle heard the word *scorpion*, he receded into his shell and said in a muffled voice, "My new friend? You cannot be serious. You are no friend of mine."

"Don't you want to be my friend? From afar, I have always admired your ability to live both on land and water. Just give me a chance, will you? Let me show you what a good friend I can be," said the scorpion in tears.

The turtle's heart melted, and he said, "Okay. We can be friends. I do not like to see anybody crying."

The scorpion wiped his tears and said quietly, "If you are my friend, prove it by taking me across the watering hole to the other side."

"No, no. I cannot do that. I cannot swim without bringing my neck, my head, and my feet out of my shell. If I do so, you will sting me," said the turtle.

"You misunderstand me. I could never hurt a friend, and you are now my friend. You must trust me." The scorpion again started weeping.

The turtle relented and said, "I did not mean to upset you. Okay. Well, it is time for me to go back into the water. I am too warm. Hop onto my back and hold tight as we make the crossing." The scorpion did so.

Into the water went the turtle, and he began swimming. Just as he reached the marshy area on the other side where many grasses grew, the scorpion stung the turtle on the neck and slid onto the nearest blade of grass.

Struggling to make it to the bank, the turtle gave the scorpion a look of betrayal and said, "I thought we were friends. How could you do this to me?"

The scorpion laughed and said, "I stung you because I thought that you might dive under the water and drown me."

Since that day, the turtle has never trusted the scorpion.

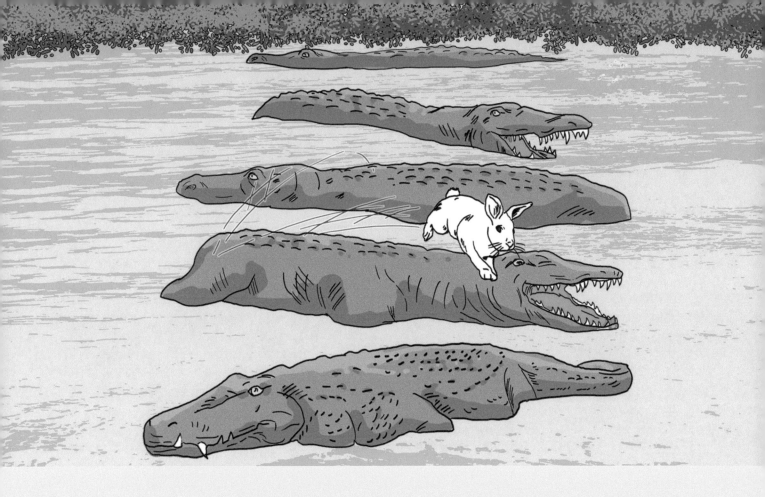

5. The Wise and Cunning Rabbit

On an island in the middle of Amasu River, a tributary of the Cross River, the only inhabitants were a wise old man and a poor rabbit. The island was full of rocks and giant boulders, and there was not a single tree or a blade of grass to be found anywhere. The rabbit scoured the island for food but could find none. He was very hungry. He sat on the shore and looked out at the opposite shore, where he saw a wide expanse of greenery. With his telescope, he saw many fat rabbits frolicking about and enjoying the abundance of the land. He became agitated. He sidled up to the wise old man sunning himself on a cane chaise longue and sat down with a glum face.

The man said, "Hey, neighbor. What's up? You look unhappy. You should be enjoying the beautiful breeze and sunshine in this paradise."

The rabbit's stomach growled, and he thought, *How can I enjoy anything on an empty stomach?*

The old man persisted, saying, "Tell me, what is wrong? I am sure I can solve your problem no matter what it is."

By this time, the rabbit was shaking with hunger and had doubled up in pain. "There is no food here for me," he whined. "I need grass. Look over there." He pointed to the far shore. "My fellow rabbits are living in luxury. What I would give to go and join them!"

The wise old man cast his eyes on the rabbit and said, "Your problem has a very easy solution."

Immediately, the rabbit forgot his stomach pains stomach and said, "Please, sir, tell me. I am very anxious. My situation is desperate, and I will surely die if I continue to live here."

The old man said, "I suggest you either swim across or row across in a canoe. These are the two options left to you."

On hearing this, the rabbit leaped up and scoured the island for a canoe since he could not swim, but there was no canoe and no trees out of which he could fashion one. He did not know what to do. He sat at the edge of the water pondering his fate. Then he saw a big head with large bright eyes, a large mouth, and sharp teeth. It was the crocodile coming to shore to sun himself. The rabbit scrambled as far away as he could to avoid contact with the ferocious-looking animal. Then a thought came to his head: *Why not ask the crocodile the best way to cross over? After all, crocodiles live between the two shores.*

As soon as the crocodile emerged from the water and lay lazily sunning himself, the rabbit felt confident enough to approach. He said, "Hey, big man, did you have a nice swim today? The water must be a bit warm."

The crocodile did not stir but replied, "I had a vigorous swim and am tired. I need my rest. Please go away." Then he raised his big head.

Frightened, the rabbit jumped as far away as possible. After about ten minutes, the rabbit came back and said, "My, my, you crocodiles are really big."

"Of course we are big. What do you think? Can't you see?" replied the crocodile proudly.

"That makes it easy for anyone to see how many crocodiles there are," said the rabbit.

"I know we are many, but I do not really know how many we are. It has never occurred to us to find out," said the crocodile.

"Well, my dear friend, I can assure you that knowing how many of you there are can be quite helpful, especially in times of danger, such as when you are being hunted. If you know how many of you have been killed, you will know when it is time for you to leave the area."

"Ah! My friend, you are right," said the crocodile. "Only two days ago, some men came and took the lives of several of us. I heard them say they needed the skin for shoes. I really do not know how many crocodiles are left because we cannot count."

"Let me help you. I know how to count. Tell all your friends to come here and form a line from this shore to that shore. I will then count them and tell you how many are left."

The crocodile thought about this but continued his rest without saying a word. Soon, it was time for him to swim to the other side. The rabbit sat on the beach looking longingly at the opposite shore. His stomach growled, and he wondered whether the crocodile would remember him after he had reunited with his friends. Lost in thought and preoccupied with his stomach, he almost missed what was happening. Looking up, he saw all the crocodiles in a long line that stretched from one shore to the other. At first, he could not believe his eyes. Then he quickly composed himself and jumped onto the nose of the first crocodile, ran along its back to its tail, and jumped onto the nose of the next one. Standing on the back of the last one, he shouted, "Only twenty left." On he went until he had reached the green land on the other side. He skipped off to join his fellow rabbits feasting on the abundance of green grass. In the land of the rabbits, he was noted as cunning and wise.

6. The Blackbird and the Vulture

One day in the animal kingdom, a call went out from the chief of the feathered ones to all birds to celebrate the crowning of their new mighty ruler in a month. In preparation for the event, the birds strutted around cleaning and washing their plumes. One blackbird called Akula was a bit unsure of herself.

One of the events on the day of the celebration was a beauty contest. The beautiful egret with its long neck and dazzling white feathers had entered, and Akula was sure she would not stand a chance of winning. Standing next to the egret, she felt dirty and ugly. She needed to improve her appearance. As the day of the contest approached, she went about with long and face, unsure of what to do. As she perched on a branch of an iroko tree, a vulture joined her. The vulture had just eaten rotten meat that he found near the market, and Akula could smell the foul odor. She contemplated flying away, but then the vulture said, "My friend, are you going to the festival next month?"

"I am not sure," said Akula. "What chance will I have in the beauty competition against the egret or the parrot or even the cock and the duck? They all have beautiful colors in their feathers. Try as I might, I am only a blackbird." At this point, she turned and searched for insects to catch because she was hungry.

"What nonsense!" said the vulture in a very satisfied tone. "You only need to use soap and water to wash away that charcoal on your feathers. You will be surprised how gloriously white you will be if you wash every day for a week. You will be as white as the egret." He turned his head and belched.

Akula moved farther from him to avoid the stench. Then, thinking that perhaps the vulture was telling the truth, she said, "Are you sure?" Akula pecked at a worm she spotted inside a crack in the branch.

"Of course I am sure," said the vulture.

Off Akula went to the market, where she purchased soap, a brush, and a sponge. Every day, she immersed herself in water and scrubbed her plumage. She scrubbed and scrubbed so hard that many of her feathers fell out.

When they saw her, one of her friends said, "Akula! Are you sick? You do not look as healthy as you used to." Another said, "Perhaps you need to see a doctor."

She scoffed at them, saying, "There is nothing wrong with me. I am working very hard to prepare for the festival."

She persisted with her scrubbing, and by the seventh day, she had no feathers, and her body was covered with bloody sores.

"This is not working," she said to herself. "Perhaps I am doing it all wrong. I need to go back and talk to the vulture."

She went back to the iroko tree in despair and perched on the branch, hoping to consult her vulture friend to learn what she had done wrong. As soon as the stinking vulture arrived, Akula the blackbird beckoned him to come near, but the flies that had followed the vulture descended on her.

She cried out in despair, "Please tell me what I have done wrong! I washed every day as you said to, but now, as you can see, all my feathers are gone and I am covered with sores."

The vulture laughed and said, "It takes hard work to be beautiful and to stay that way. Do not despair. New feathers will come in, and they will be as beautiful and white as those of the egret. You will see."

Since the festival was still a few weeks away, Akula felt she still had time to become beautiful, so she concentrated on putting salves on her wounds and keeping them clean.

As the day approached and her new feathers appeared, she examined them for changes in their color. Lo and behold, they were the same old black color, only now instead of being a rich black, they were a dull, ugly grayish black. Akula was crushed. She could not possibly go to the festival looking like that. It seemed that all her effort to change her color had come to naught.

She had been misled by the stinking vulture, who was jealous of her shiny black feathers. Sitting out of the contest, she cursed the vulture. From that day forth, she vowed to be satisfied with her natural attributes, not to wish to be what she was not, and to avoid deceitful friends.

7. The Spider and the Elephant

In all the animal kingdom, the elephant was strongest and biggest. Mr. Elephant was proud of his size and strength and never hesitated in boasting about them to all and sundry. One day, as he walked along the jungle, felling trees and causing havoc in the forest as he went, a spider descended from a tree and hurried to get out of the elephant's way. The elephant, full of himself for being the king of the jungle, was totally unaware of what lay underfoot and almost squashed the spider.

The spider cried out, "Look where you are going! You are not the only one in this forest."

"I do not have to look," said the elephant. "I am the king of all I survey. Little things like you should get out of my way."

"Well," said the spider, "you may be big and strong, but I can tell you that I am cleverer and faster than you."

The elephant roared with laughter, and the jungle shook with his noise. Then he said, "It is no contest. Of course I will win any competition that both of us enter. I am, after all, the biggest animal in the jungle. You!" He laughed again. "Nobody can see since you are so small."

"Shall we set a date for the competition since you are so sure that you will win?" said the spider.

The elephant laughed even more uproariously and agreed to a date. Both animals went home to prepare for the nine-kilometer race. The elephant was so sure of his victory that he slept as soon as he got home, and when he woke, he told his relatives and neighbors that the race was going to be a piece of cake and urged them to come to the venue at the appointed time.

When the spider arrived home, he called a meeting of all his relatives. He selected nine of his brothers who looked exactly like him and walked the length of the course with them, placing one of his brothers at the starting line and the other eight at the end of each kilometer. He told them that as soon as they saw the elephant approach, they should sprint ahead of him. He went to the end of the course and spun a web.

When the race started, the elephant ran as fast as he could, but to his surprise, at the first kilometer mark, the spider was in front of him. He ran faster and faster, but at each kilometer marker, the spider was already ahead of him. The faster he ran, the faster it seemed the spider ran, as he was always a step ahead. As he approached the finish line, he spied the spider sprinting across the line. He was angry and rushed forward, but he became entangled in the web. Try as he might, he could not extricate himself because the clever spider was busy spinning an intricate web around his trunk. The elephant thrashed about, knocking down trees. In the end, he became very tired, and his breathing slowed, and he lay down. He was forced to admit that the spider was faster and cleverer than he.

8. The Friendship between the Cock and the Fox

In a small hamlet in the forest next to a village in the kingdom of Eze Chi, there lived a cock whom all the animals feared because they believed he carried fire on his head. This was the source of his beauty and power. He liked to strut around frightening the hens and small chicks, showing off his flaming comb. All the animals in the surrounding forest believed that if they came near him, the fire surrounding his head would consume them.

The cock was jealous of the other animals who had many friends with whom they passed the time. On market days, as soon as the cock arrived, all the other animals dispersed and gave him a wide berth. He could not understand why no one wanted to be his friend. At home, he sat outside the henhouse lost in thought, wondering what he had done to deserve such a lonely life.

He was particularly fond of one hen, and he knew she was not afraid of him, so he sought her out and said, "I went to the market the other day. As soon as I appeared, all the animals ran away from me. I cannot understand it. I do not bite like the snake, and I do not want to kill them like the fox, leopard, and hyena. I do not sting like the scorpion. Do you know why everyone is afraid of me?"

The hen thought and thought and scratched at the ground, looking for a worm.

It seemed like she had not heard what the cock had said, so he asked, "You are not afraid of me, are you?"

The hen raised her head and looked at the cock. "We hens are happy that the animals are afraid of you. Have you noticed that when you sit outside the henhouse, no animal who might kill us will approach? You keep us safe from the fox and the snake in particular."

"But I like the fox," the cock said. "I want to be friends with him."

"Oh well," said the hen. "Suit yourself. We do not like the fox."

Just then, the cock saw a fox from afar, so he shouted, "Hi, Mr. Fox! Come and talk to me. I want to be friends."

The fox backed away, saying, "Please leave me alone. I do not want to be consumed."

"Consumed?" said the cock."What do you mean? I do not eat flesh like you do."

The fox shouted, "You may not eat meat, but if I come near you, that thing on your head will burn me up and make it possible for you to eat me!"

The cock laughed uproariously. He turned and looked inside the henhouse, where all the hens were gathered listening to the conversation and wondering whether the cock had any brains.

"He does not care about us," one of them muttered. "If he did, he would not want to be friends with the fox."

The cock ignored the muttering, saying to himself that the hens just wanted to keep him for themselves. Then he said to the fox, "Why do you think I will roast you and eat you? I am not hot."

The fox laughed. "You are a crafty animal. I know for sure that that thing you carry on your head is fire and that once I come near you, it will burn me up. Then you and your brood of hens will enjoy a feast."

The cock thought for a minute before replying, "But, my friend, I am not carrying fire. What you see on my head is my comb. It is what distinguishes me from a hen and makes me special. Come near and touch it."

The fox hesitated, and the hens shouted in unison, "He is lying to you! He is carrying fire. Do not come near!"

This made the cock really angry, and he frightened the hens away. Then he turned to the fox and said, "Do not mind the hens; they are jealous of any new friends I make. They want to keep me for themselves. I am really telling you the truth."

The cock and the fox stared at each other for a while, and finally, the fox said, "Maybe you are telling the truth. Will you let me touch your comb? If what you say is true, we can be friends."

The Cock replied, "Come, then, and see for yourself."

The fox slowly approached the cock, raised a paw, and touched the cock's comb, saying, "Dear friend, I am glad you encouraged me to come near. This is an honor."

But before the cock could answer, the fox pounced on him and bit him off his head, thus killing him. The hens were aghast as they saw the fox tear the cock apart. They ran as far inside the henhouse as possible. One of them said, "He should have known that the fox is our natural enemy. It serves him right for not listening."

The farmer heard the commotion and ran after the fox, who escaped. To safeguard his hens, he enclosed them in a safer coop with a more secure door.

9. Why the Tortoise Has Markings on Its Shell

In years gone by, all flying animals were governed by the king of the air. He was a powerful person worshipped by everything that travels above, including flies, dragonflies, butterflies, and birds of every species. One day not long ago, the king issued a proclamation inviting everyone in his domain to an important feast commemorating his ascension to the throne. As usual for such occasions, the king of the air decorated the sky with vibrant pinks, purples, reds, blues, and grays and rainbows crossing from east to west and north to south. It was a sight to behold. All the land animals marveled at the sky's beauty, and many were jealous of the flying animals because they were the ones chosen to enjoy such beauty up close. While several animals were content to enjoy the sight from a distance, only the tortoise allowed his jealousy to overcome him. Sitting in his corner under an iroko tree that sheltered him from the rain, he spied a colorful bird perched on a drooping branch.

"Are you going to the feast?" asked the tortoise.

"Of course I will be going," twittered the bird.

Just then, a swallowtail with unusually bright colors flew up and perched nearby. So the tortoise turned to him and said, "I presume you, too, will be going."

"To what?" inquired the butterfly, his voice full of surprise.

"The feast! I meant the one that all you lucky flying things have been invited to. Don't tell me you were not also invited?" replied the tortoise.

"I have been thinking about it," said the swallowtail, "but you know, it is being held in a very high place. We flying insects may have difficulty flying all the way up there. Tell me, Mr. T, are you thinking of going?"

"How can I? I do not have wings. It is impossible for me to leave the ground," replied Mr. Tortoise angrily. "But I would really like to go."

Just then, a whole flock of different birds and a swarm of insects descended on the iroko tree. The branches bent under the weight of so many birds and insects eager to talk about the wonders that awaited them in the air palace.

During the ensuing discussion, Mr. Praying Mantis said, "For my part, I have never been near the king's palace. I am sure I will get lost, but I want very much to go. I wish I could find someone to carry me up."

The tortoise saw an opening, so he said, "I would like to help, but unfortunately, I cannot fly. I have always wished that I had wings and feathers. Many of you have such beautiful colors on your wings and bodies. I envy that you can fly up to the heavens and see places that I will never get to see."

All the birds present said in chorus, "If you want to go to the feast, we can lend you some of our feathers and can craft wings for you."

"Will you do that for me?" replied the tortoise, his voice trembling. "It would be fantastic if I could just lift up and follow all of you to the palace in the sky. I would forever be grateful to all of you, my friends."

The birds conferred among themselves, and each agreed to contribute some feathers to make it possible for the tortoise's wish to come true. Then, they had to find a way to fix the feathers to the tortoise. They scratched their heads and thought and thought. Suddenly, an answer came from a small yellow butterfly who had been following the discussion.

She said loudly, "I know what you need."

Everyone's heads swiveled in her direction. The place was quiet.

Then she said, "Remember the rubber tree close by? Its sap is very sticky. I myself try to avoid it since one of my friends perched on the sticky liquid from the rubber tree and was unable to free herself. Perhaps we can use that liquid."

This long statement from the yellow butterfly made her tired, and she folding her wings and fell asleep, despite the chattering of the birds.

A big hawk nearby said, "She is right. I have once gotten my talons stuck in the rubber sap. It took quite a lot of strength to free myself. Let's give it a try."

A nearby kite then ventured to say, "We need to hurry up. It is quite a long way to the palace. Let's collect the feathers and head to the rubber tree. You, Tortoise, should quickly follow us. It's just round the bend from where we are now."

When they arrived at the base of the rubber tree, each bird dipped its prettiest feather into the sap and pasted it on the tortoise. When the task was completed and the Tortoise lifted off the ground, the contributors expected the tortoise to shout with joy. Instead, his countenance was dark. He looked extremely uncomfortable.

The birds were surprised by this. They consulted one another and decided that the hawk should be their spokesperson to find out what was troubling the tortoise. The hawk asked all those present perched on the ground to form a wide circle around the tortoise. He then stepped inside the circle, looked up, and said, "We have given you what you wanted. Why are you still sad?"

The tortoise stuck his head and neck out and said, "I have one more request. Despite your kindness in providing me with wings and feathers, the king will know at once that I am not one of you and will not let me into the palace."

"Why not?" said the feathered animals in unison. "You now look like us."

"But, to enter the palace, one has to be announced. My given name is Tortoise, and that surely will expose me as an interloper."

"Oh! We see what you mean," said the praying mantis, looking down at the tortoise.

Then, the hawk, who was frantic because he had spied a dead zebra nearby and wanted his share of the meat, said, "Tortoise is your given name. There is nothing we can do about that."

As he turned to leave, the tortoise said, "Well, perhaps we can solve the problem by my taking another name temporarily."

"What name would you like?" said the crow, who also was a bit tired of the show and wanted to get off so he could conserve his strength for the journey to the air palace.

The tortoise, who was sitting in their midst, closed his eyes. After a minute, he thought he would need a name that would give him an advantage over all the flying animals, so he said, "Since I have feathers from each one of you, perhaps I should be called All Of You. That is a good name."

After a little discussion, the flying animals quickly agreed to the new name.

On the day of the festivities, the tortoise led the retinue of flying animals to the palace and was welcomed warmly by the king of the air. The tables were heaped with food and drinks.

In his prepared speech, the king said, "I am very glad that you, my subjects, have come from far and wide to rejoice with me. This food is for all of you. Please enjoy." He then turned and left.

Since the tortoise had assumed the name All Of You, the birds and insects assumed that the king meant that the food was for the tortoise alone, so they sat looking at the food while the tortoise consumed everything on the table without offering them a morsel. What he could not eat, he stored in a bag to eat later.

All the birds were angry, and in a conference, they decided on a just punishment for his selfishness. As they were about to depart and were in midair, the kite shouted, "Now is the time for one and all to take back your feathers!"

Each bird descended on the tortoise during the flight and took back all the feathers. The Tortoise went into free fall.

"Help! Help!" the tortoise shouted. "Please help me! I am going to die!"

The birds ignored him. He fell to earth, and his shell broke into pieces. He begged the animals passing by to help him protect his skin from all the hazards around, but none would come to his aid because they knew him as a crafty animal who used his friends for his own good.

In his anguish, he begged a passing snail, "My friend, you, too, have shell, and you must know the danger I am in without mine. Please help me."

The snail knew that without his shell, the tortoise would be exposed to the elements and would be an easy target for crows, insects, and other animals, so he collected pieces of his shell and glued them to the tortoise with his slimy saliva. That is why all tortoises have patchwork shells.

10. The Great Famine

A long time ago, when all the animals lived happily together sharing the plentiful food, a soothsayer lived among them. One day, he summoned all the animals to his compound, and the animals came from far and wide because of his fame in predicting the future—nine out of ten of his predictions came true. When all the animals had arrived, the soothsayer stood on a platform in their midst.

He glared at his audience and said loudly, "My fellow beings, I see a sad time in front of us. I know at this time we are enjoying the bounty of the land, and it is difficult for us to imagine, but I tell you, in the not so distant future, all this abundance will be gone. The rains will stop, the rivers will dry up, the grass will wither, and we will have nothing to eat. So I urge you to prepare now for that time. Mark my words, we will have famine. It will come as ordained."

The animals stared at him in disbelief."What is he talking about?" one of them murmured. "Look outside. Everywhere you look there is food. We are even not able to eat it all."

At one point, the elephant raised his trunk and shouted, "Do not listen to him! Not all his predictions happen. Remember last year when he called a meeting to announce that the sun would go dark for a long time? Did it happen? It is plain that we have everything we want and more. I prophesy that this good life will continue forever."

The soothsayer shouted back, "Listen to me! Prepare for the worst! It may not happen in the immediate future, but it will happen. We will suffer the worst famine ever. I urge all of you to start hoarding your food now. Build a secret barn and store as much as you can. My fellow beings, I urge you to pay attention. My words will come to pass."

Unfortunately, the elephant's words carried the day, and the animals continued to waste food and water. The only animal that reflected on what the soothsayer said was Mama Squirrel, who felt that there was a kernel of truth in his words, so she prepared for the famine. With the help of her children, she built an underground nest in which she stored yam, palm fruits, cocoyam, groundnuts and other assorted nuts and seeds, various fruits, and pots of water.

After several years of plenty, the time came when the rain ceased to fall, and the land experienced a protracted dry period. No food would grow, and the rivers dried up. The animals had to roam far for food. Only Mama Squirrel had food in her underground barn.

She called her family together and said, "We are lucky to have food, and I do not want to give it away. So, access to this hole will be limited to those who can whisper a secret code. Before I give you the code, you must promise under penalty of banishment that you will not disclose the code to any living animal."

Her daughters quickly swore that they would not disclose the code, and Mama Squirrel told it to them. Every day, she sent her daughters out to see what was happening, and when they came back, they would utter the secret code and run into their home. The starving animals above were very jealous of the plump little squirrels.

Soon all the animals moved away in search of water, but the tortoise stayed behind and lived off of dry leaves, insects, and nuts that he found in the droppings of other animals. When the tortoise saw the plump squirrel children playing outside their hole, he surmised that their mother had prepared for the famine and had stored plenty of food underground. He knocked on the squirrel hole's door.

"Mama Squirrel!" he cried. "I am the only animal still here. Everyone has gone in search of water. There is no food anywhere. Please take pity on me and give me a morsel to eat."

Mama Squirrel peeped out to see who was at the door. "Mr. Tortoise," she said, "I have only enough food for myself and my children. I have none to spare. Why don't you run along with the other animals? Perhaps there will be food beyond our shores." She quickly latched the door and went to her bed to rest.

The tortoise was disappointed, but he quickly thought of a scheme to lay his hands on the treasure inside the hole. He positioned himself near the hole and listened to the squirrel children as they let themselves in.

He heard one of the squirrels sing:

Mother Squirrel, good Mother,

Quickly, quickly,

Open the door, open the door.

Your child is hungry, hungry, hungry!

Open the door!

Your child is hungry, I say, hungry.

The next day, just as the squirrel children came out to play, the tortoise crawled near the hole's opening and sang the song he had heard.

Mama Squirrel heard the words, but the melody was off. Suspicious, she peeped through the keyhole and saw her children still playing outside, so she did not open the door.

After his ruse failed that first time, the tortoise lingered near the hole for months, listened to the little squirrels, and practiced emulating their voices. When he had been reduced to skin and bones, he approached the hole again, and this time, Mama Squirrel opened the door, and he rushed in. A fight ensued, but there was no way Mama Squirrel could win since the tortoise retracted into his shell whenever she tried to beat him. Soon, tired from the fight, Mama Squirrel went to a corner and slept. This gave the tortoise the opportunity to carry off all the food in the hole.

Just as he was taking away the last load of food, he dropped a juicy palm fruit, and it fell back into the hole just as Mama Squirrel woke up. She rushed after the fruit, which was her favorite food, but it fell into another hole nearby. Mama Squirrel dived after it. Lo and behold, the fruit landed on a table in the palace of the spirit of the underworld.

"What is this? An unexpected gift?" cried the spirit of the underworld, who was at that time composing a proclamation to the new subjects he had acquired in his realm because the famine elsewhere. "Yum yum." He smacked his lips and bit into the juicy flesh of the palm fruit. He had never tasted such a fruit, so he turned to the squirrel, who was standing aghast at this unexpected turn of events, and said, "Thank you for this precious gift! Nobody has ever given me such a gift. Yum yum."

The squirrel guffawed and said, "You are welcome." She turned to hide the tears of disappointment that sprang to her eyes.

The spirit stopped her as she started walking back the way she came and said, "Tell me, Mother Squirrel, is there anything I can do for you? You only have to ask for it, and it will be yours."

Mama Squirrel wiped her tears, gulped, and said, "M-m-most feared spirit of the underworld," another gulp, "m-m-my only request is that you should bless me so that my family and I will always have enough food to eat."

"Come here, Mother Squirrel!" the spirit said so loudly that those above heard something that sounded like a thunderbolt.

Mama Squirrel bowed her head and slowly approached.

The spirit placed his big hands on her and said, "I grant you your request. None of your family will ever lack food. "

It was a happy squirrel that returned to her family. Since then, even when there is famine in the land, squirrels always manage to have enough to eat.

11. Who Is the Strongest of Us All?

The forest shook as the elephant walked to the water hole. He was running late.

"Oh my," he said to himself. "I bet the place will be packed by now. I hate it when the water hole is crowded because I have to avoid stepping on all the small animals scurrying around. I do not know why they cannot step aside for us big ones. I think I will raise this issue during the next meeting of all the animals in the plain."

As he walked along, he blew his horn to signal the animals to step away from the road.

"Out of my way! Out of my way! I might step on you. Out of my way!" he shouted.

The small animals scurried away because they did not want to be trampled, but the tortoise refused to step aside. He stood his ground, daring the elephant to step on him. This was exactly what happened. Fortunately, he was not crushed. So, emboldened, he said to the elephant, "You think you are the king of the forest, and you boast of your strength all the time. But you stood on me and could not crush me. See? There is not a dent on my carapace. In actual fact, I am stronger than you."

The elephant looked down at the tortoise, laughed, and said, "I do not have time for your nonsense. I am in a hurry. I am very thirsty and hot. We can talk about who is the strongest another time."

"I understand," said the tortoise. "But we need to settle this at some point, so I suggest that we meet tomorrow morning on top of the nearest hill to test our strength."

"Which hill?" asked the elephant.

"The one just before the river. I know we call it a water hole, but it is really a river, you know."

"All right, then. I will see you tomorrow. I am eager to settle the matter once and for all."

The elephant continued his journey. He was the last animal to arrive at the water hole. Most of the animals had had their fill of water and had started their journeys home. Only the hippo and some crocodiles were still there, and they rested on the shore.

After drinking his fill, the elephant returned home. At home, he told his wife and children of the tortoise's ridiculous suggestion. They all laughed and wondered at the stupidity of the tortoise to think that he was stronger than the elephant, as everybody knew the elephant was the king of the forest. Little did they know what the tortoise was planning.

As soon as the sun made its appearance on the eastern sky the next day, the tortoise ran to the water hole, and there the hippos were returning from their nightly scrounging for food along the shore line. He said to a male hippo who was just about to dive into the water, "Please, Mr. Hippo, stop and listen."

"Go away you rascal tortoise," said the hippo. "You are nothing but trouble."

"No, no, I really have something important to tell you."

The hippo lay on the sand and rolled about before saying, "Okay, but it had better be important. I am eager to get back into the water."

The tortoise squinted, screwed up his face, and said in a solemn tone, "I have been watching you. You are not really as strong as you look. I bet I am stronger than you."

"What nonsense is this?" shouted the hippo. "Get away from here immediately before I crush you!"

The tortoise responded sweetly, "Why don't I prove it? Let's have a tug of war. The animal who wins will be declared the strongest."

The hippo laughed and laughed, but nonetheless, he agreed. He called all the other hippos to come and watch him defeat the tortoise.

The tortoise found a rope, handed the hippo one end, and said, "I will be at the top of the hill. The giraffe is the referee. When he cries, 'Begin!', you pull."

By this time, the sun had begun to brighten the plain. The tortoise went up the hill, where the elephant was already sitting under a tree, waiting for him impatiently. The elephant was surrounded by many animals equally eager to know the outcome of the contest.

"Hey, sir, I am sorry I am late," said the tortoise. "I brought a rope. You hold one end, and I will run down the hill with the other end. The giraffe will be our referee. When I am in position, I will give him a sign to indicate that I am ready. As soon as he says, 'Begin!', both of us will pull the rope. The animal who moves the other will be declared the winner."

The elephant was quite sure that he would win, so he quickly agreed. The tortoise ran down to a spot where neither the hippo nor the elephant could see him and gave a sign to the giraffe, who shouted, "Begin!"

The hippo and the elephant each pulled and pulled, but neither could move the other. After thirty minutes, both competitors gave up. The giraffe declared that both were of equal strength, and both agreed that the tortoise was as strong as they were. Since that day, all the animals have held the tortoise in very high regard.

12. The Tortoise and the Ostrich

A long time ago, when all the animals lived together on a big plain, the tortoise no friends. All the animals despised him because of his cunning and deceitful ways. He was very lonely. He longed to have just one friend with whom he could play and discuss his problems without judgment. He asked many animals for their friendship, but most held a grudge for their last dealings with him. The squirrel remembered that he deceived her into thinking that he was her daughter during the famine. The birds and flying insects remembered how selfish he was when they invited him to visit the king of the air.

In despair, the tortoise approached the ostrich, who had feathers and was a bird, had never learned how to fly. He knew that many birds despised the ostrich because he was so ungainly. The chickens hated him because he ate large quantities of food and did not like to socialize with them. So the tortoise bided his time, and when he spied the ostrich strutting alone not far from the iroko tree in a corner of the Amasu village, he ran up and said, "Hi! How are you? I see we are all alone here."

The ostrich looked down, wondering who was talking to him. He saw a big fat worm and gobbled it up. As he raised his head, he saw the tortoise looking at him expectantly. The tortoise repeated his question, and the ostrich responded, "Are you talking to me?"

"Of course. Nobody is here but the two of us," said the tortoise.

"What do you want with me?" said the ostrich. He looked around for another worm to gobble but saw instead kernels of corn that had fallen out of a trader's bag as he carried it to the market. Overjoyed, he strutted over to gobble them up before those nasty hens saw them.

In his warmest voice, the tortoise said, "I just want to be your friend. One needs a friend, and since we are both without friends, we should team up. Together, I am sure we can overcome any adversity."

The ostrich raised his head again and saw tears in the tortoise's eyes. He was moved and wanted very much to stop the tortoise from crying, as he could not abide tears, so he said, "Loosen up! If it will make you happy, I can be your friend."

The tortoise wiped his tears and said, "Are you serious? You will be my friend?"

"That is what I said. Can't you hear?" said the ostrich, a bit flustered.

"I am so happy. I really need a friend," replied the Tortoise excitedly. It is so much easier to do farm work if you have a friend with you. Don't you think?"

The ostrich went back to pecking at the grass and strutting about. He had the reputation for burying his head in the sand, thus being indifferent to what was happening around him. So, the tortoise had to come up with a plan to energize the ostrich to act for the benefit of the friendship. He formed one, and the next day, as soon as he woke up, the tortoise went to visit his friend the ostrich.

As usual, the ostrich had his head in the sand to look for scraps and was unaware of the tortoise until he nudged the ostrich's leg.

"Don't do that! You will cause me to tumble," the ostrich said, kicking the tortoise.

"I just want to tell you that I am visiting," the tortoise said. "We are friends, aren't we? Friends visit each other often."

"Okay, then. Did you have a nice rest last night?" mumbled the Ostrich as he continued his quest for worms.

"Hey, friend, why do you spend so much time looking for food? It is planting season and if we band together and plant, by harvest time we will have enough to carry us over the next hungry season. We are lucky in that our patches of land are next to each other, so it will be quite easy for us to combine our efforts." The words tumbled from the tortoise's lips in his excitement.

"What do you mean by combining our efforts? I get everything I want without exerting much effort," retorted the Ostrich. My patch is next to the road, and farmers drop a lot of grains and waste here every day. I just have to sit here and food often falls on my lap."

"But, my friend, it will not always be easy for you to get the food you want since I heard that they are building a new road on the other side of the plain that will connect all the farm land. This road next to your patch will no longer be in use."

"Oh, I have not heard of the new road. When is it going to be completed?"

"Soon," said the tortoise.

The ostrich thought about this. He had not thought of cultivating his land this season. He was quite happy picking at the food dropped by careless farmers returning from their farms. Besides, it was hard work to dig and plant corn and other crops. But on the other hand, perhaps his friend the tortoise, who was more conversant with the ways of the world, knew what he was talking about. And this new road! The ostrich had never heard of it. Perhaps it was wise for them to work together. Who knew? Perhaps at harvest time, they would have plenty of food. It would be nice to store some for the hungry period when the plants had not yet matured and farmers hardly wasted any food. They could even sell the surplus to lazy animals. All these thoughts swirling around the ostrich's brain tired him, so he went back to digging for grubs.

The next day, the tortoise came back to nudge the ostrich into making a decision because the rains would soon come, so the plants needed to be planted within a few days. He was pleasantly surprised when the ostrich quickly said, "Let's do it."

That was how it came about that the tortoise and the ostrich planted a big farm with cocoyam, yam, maize, assorted legumes and nuts, and a type of beans called okpodudu, which was highly valued in the area. That year, their barn was full, and for years, they fed off its abundance.

In the fifth year of their friendship, the tortoise noticed that the barn was becoming empty. After the initial planting, the ostrich had been unwilling to exert any effort to replant any of the crops in subsequent years, so, after surveying the food in the barn, the tortoise decided that the only way he would have enough food to last him for another year was to deprive the ostrich of food. To this end, he scrounged around the barn for left over okpodudu beans, which had become the ostrich's favorite food, and cooked them with all the spices he could find.

The aroma of the beans enticed the ostrich to lift his head and strut to the simmering pot. "Eh, friend, what's cooking? It smells delicious. Give me some!" The Ostrich smacked his lips in anticipation.

"Not so fast. You have to pronounce the name of the food before you can eat it." The tortoise scooped a spoonful of okpodudu into his mouth.

"But," said the ostrich, "this is ridiculous. You know I cannot pronounce the name. Is that why you insist on this silly rule?"

"At least try to pronounce it. How can you say that you cannot pronounce it when you have not even tried?" said the tortoise disparagingly.

The ostrich tried, but it came out as, "Kpo-kpo-dudu … du-kpo … ikpo-dudu … ikpo—"

The tortoise laughed uproariously. "No food for you, my friend. Go away and practice."

Unfortunately, try as the ostrich might, the words came out wrong. He looked on helplessly as the tortoise consumed the whole pot of beans.

That night, the ostrich thought of how he could punish his friend for his trick. He decided to cook the tortoise's favorite vegetable. After he had finished, he laid a beautiful table and placed the pot of food on top. He spooned some on a plate for the tortoise and then called out, "My friend, the food is ready! But before you come, make sure that you wash your hands. I cannot abide anyone who comes to the table with dirty hands."

That's easy, thought the tortoise, so he quickly washed his hands, but as he approached the table, without thinking, he placed them in the dirt. The ostrich ordered him to go and wash his hands again. The tortoise did so, but as many times as he tried, he was not able to keep his hands clean long enough to sit at the table, and the ostrich was merciless in his demand for clean hands.

Now it was the tortoise's to watch the food disappear because of a demand that he could not meet. In the end, both animals learned a valuable lesson: do to others as you would have them do to you.

13. The Old Pot and the New Pot

In a village there lived an old man who had a pot as old as he was. The pot had served him for many years and had been blackened by constant use. The old man was getting a bit tired of it and felt that he needed a replacement, but he could not summon enough strength to go to the market to buy one.

One day, he was sitting outside his house fashioning a broom when he heard a woman shout, "Okoh! Have you seen the beautiful pots on display at the village square? They are really beautiful."

On hearing this, other villagers came out of their huts and made their way to the village square to look at the pots. The old man left his broom unfinished and rushed to the site with them. A trader had had brought beautiful pots from Lokoja, on the river Niger. These were different from the pots made in the village. They were special. All were well made and painted in beautiful colors.

As the old man examined them, one pot beckoned to him, as if saying, "Buy me. You will not regret it."

So, plucking up courage, the old man bought that pot and brought it home. The old pot saw him enter with the new pot. The old man caressed the new pot and turned it around to admire it before leaving it to one side of the kitchen. The old pot saw the old man's affection for it but said nothing. The old man then left the kitchen, and the new pot looked on lovingly as he made his way across the courtyard to the main house. Seeing the look, the old pot smirked but did not utter a word.

The new pot noticed the old pot smirking, so she said, "Hi, Old Pot. What are you smirking about? Why are you sitting there looking like an old hag? Your days are over." She laughed.

The old pot surveyed the new pot's fancy painting and replied, "Say what you like. You are new and obviously inexperienced. Time will tell which of us the old man likes best."

Every day when the old man came into the kitchen, he admired the new pot but used the Old Pot to boil his yam and make his pepper soup. After cooking, he emptied the food into the new pot, tossed the old pot in the corner, and lovingly carried the new pot to the main house to eat from her. Then he gently washed her, making sure that no remnants of food remained, and reluctantly put her away. Every time this happened, the new pot gloated primly.

The old pot laughed and said, "Time will tell."

This made the new pot angry, and she replied, "I will never look as ugly as you. The old man will take very good care of me. See how he caresses me and admires me?"

"Time will tell," the old pot said. "I was new once and was treated like you. Just wait until it is your turn to be placed on the fire. It will not be easy for you to retain your luster, and once you lose it, you will be nothing. You will be treated like me."

"Rubbish!" said the new pot. "The old man loves me and will never subject me to that. He will clean and take care of me. I will never be an old blackened pot like you, fit for nothing but cooking beans and lentils."

The old pot could not help but laugh and say, "These young ones! What do they know of life? Time will tell."

As the days passed into months and the time for the New Yam Festival neared, the old man hosted so many visitors in his house that it was necessary for him to use all his pots to prepare food in. So it came about that he reluctantly used the new pot to make okra soup with chicken. He gently placed the pot on the stand over a wood fire, heated palm oil, and added sliced onions. As soon as the onion turned translucent, he dumped in chicken pieces, cut okra, spinach, crayfish, salt and pepper, and a little chicken broth. He covered the pot and let the soup simmer.

The old pot, who boiled beans nearby on another stand, eyed the new Pot and said "How are you, my friend?"

"I am fine," said the new pot, trying not to cry from the intense heat. In a trembling voice, she continued, "You think I am suffering, but you are mistaken. He loves me, and as soon as the food is done and eaten, he is going to scrub me and give me back my luster. You will see."

The old pot only shook her head, wondering at how this new crop of pots could be so gullible.

After that meal, the old man tried to clean the pew pot, but his thoughts were elsewhere, so his scrubbing was perfunctory, and he left behind some of the soot from the fire. And so it came that the old man fell into the habit of using the new pot to make stews and the old pot to boil plantain, yam, beans, and anything else that needed to be boiled. Soon, the new pot lost its luster, and then it was covered with soot. Even though the old man favored her by using her to make delicious stews, the end result was the same as it had been for the old pot, and in time, the two looked the same.

One day, the two pots sat in the corner to rest after they had been used for cooking. The new pot said to the old pot, "You were right when you said that time would tell. He hardly looks at me now."

The old pot replied, "When one is young, one never thinks of old age. I understand, my friend, and hold no grudge."

14. The Mouse and the Rat

A long time ago, when the world was young, in a village on one of the creeks of the Cross River in eastern Nigeria, several rats cohabited with the villagers. It was a rich village where people had food in abundance, and uneaten food was strewn around, so the rats who lived there were fat. When it was dark and the villagers slept, the rats, who lived in the dark corners of their homes, came out and had a field day eating the wasted food. Sometimes in the evenings, all the rats would scamper outside through the tunnels they had dug to the outskirts of the village, where the villagers dumped their waste. There, they would socialize and play.

The rats hardly come out during the day because the villagers would pursue them and kill any they could. Those rats who escaped the wrath of the villagers were likely to encounter their mortal enemies, the cats who lived in some of the houses and were ready to pounce on and kill any rat who dared come into their territory. On the whole, however, the rats had it made.

One particular rat, Mr. House Rat, lived in the house of a rich man in the village. His life was a happy one. He had plenty of food to eat because the family was particularly wasteful, and even though the family had a dog and a cat, Mr. House Rat had learned to evade them, so the animals coexisted without any problem. But Mr. House Rat had a problem: he wanted to go outside during the day and bask in the warm sun because he was getting tired of the damp and moldy room that was his home.

Sometimes when the family was away during the day, he would come out, hop onto a stool near a window, and stare out. On sunny days, he watched the children playing and marveled at the sun's rays shimmering on the zinc roofs of the well-to-do villagers' houses. He longed to frolic outside in the yard, but he was afraid of being caught and killed. On rainy days, he watched the villagers go about their business with umbrellas or big banana leaves to protect them from raindrops. On such days, he would say to himself, "What I wouldn't give to feel the rain wash away all the dirt and odor from my fur."

One sunny day, Mr. House Rat decided that he could not bear to be inside the house. He went into his storage area and pulled out his best suit with a most beautiful vest of many colors. When he was ready, he crawled through a hole and soon was outside. He felt exhilarated, so he scampered for the woods near the village for a stroll, hoping to make some friends among the animals that lived there. Enjoying the fresh air and making sure he stayed away from the paths the farmers used, he bumped into a mouse going about his business of collecting food for his family.

"Watch where you're going!" the mouse cried.

Mr. House Rat saw before him what looked like a young rat, and thinking he had hurt a child, he said with remorse, "Oh dear! I hope I have not hurt you. Where is your mother? Come here. Your mother should not have let you out of the house by yourself at your age."

"What are talking about?" said the mouse in a gruff voice. "I am going about my business, and I did not expect any of your lot to be outside at this time. Who are you?"

"I am Mr. House Rat. I live in the village, where I never have to work hard to fill my belly with food."

"I am Mr. Field Mouse. My house is under the iroko tree not far from here."

"Why are you collecting nuts?" Mr. House Rat asked.

"I don't know about you," replied Mr. Field Mouse, "but we mice love nuts and collect as many as we can this time of year to store them for the hungry months, when none of the nuts fall off the trees."

"Hmm," said Mr. House Rat. "That must be hard work, and all that work must be why your growth has been stunted. I am glad we house rats do not have to work so hard. I tell you, my friend, if you lived in my village, you would become plump in no time."

"How do you get your food, then?" asked Mr. Field Mouse.

"Food is just there for the picking. It is always available," replied Mr. House Rat smugly.

The field mouse stopped and thought a little, and then he turned to his new friend and said, "Why don't you come and see where we live? My family will welcome the distraction."

Mr. House Rat readily agreed and trailed behind Mr. Field Mouse, who by this time had filled his basked with nuts, and he dragged it on a string. Soon, they came to the large iroko tree. Mr. Field Mouse pushed aside some leaves to expose a hole, and he tossed in his basket of nuts and tumbled in. Mr. House Rat followed suit.

Inside the large hole, eight baby mice were sleeping in a corner. Mrs. Field Mouse welcomed Mr. House Rat and showed him around. She offered him some nuts as refreshment, and Mr. House Rat had some.

Before departing, he drew Mr. Mouse aside and said, "My dear friend, I must be honest with you. I think you need to move. This house is not fit for habitation. When it rains, what do you do?" Without waiting for a response, he went on, "Don't tell me. I can see for myself that you move deeper into the hole and perhaps find leaves to cover the entrance. What a lot of work! Where I live, we do not have to strain ourselves. Everything is taken care of for us."

Mr. Field Mouse was astounded by what he had heard. He thought, *Why should I work so hard when there is a paradise just beyond the woods? I should at least go and see it.* Then he said, "May be I should come and visit you for a day before I decide whether I like your life. I'm ready to visit now, if you don't mind."

So, Mr. House Rat took Mr. Field Mouse to the village. It was twilight, and the villagers were home eating their supper before bedtime. At the dump outside the village, Mr. House Rat introduced Mr. Field Mouse to his neighbors and to his many married sons and daughters.

After the social hour, the two friends made their way to the rich man's house where Mr. House Rat lived. Mr. Field Mouse congratulated Mr. House Rat on his fine home. He was impressed by how dry the house was, considering that it had been pouring with rain the whole day. He was amazed by all the food on the table, and he moved to rush toward it, but Mr. House Rat restrained him.

"I usually eat after the family has eaten," he said. "It is only polite that you allow the hand that feeds you to eat first."

"But I am hungry," said Mr. Field Mouse, and he dashed from their hiding place in the corner and jumped up unto the table. On seeing what looked like the rat, the family jumped up from the table. The father ran for a broom and pursued the animal.

Mr. Field Mouse ran for dear life, and only by sheer luck did he manage to escape into Mr. House Rat's tunnel.

Mr. House Rat caught up with him and said, "You should have waited until they had finished their meal and gone upstairs. There is always enough left for us."

By this time Mr. Field Mouse was trembling with fear. He was afraid to go back into the house, but Mr. House Rat persuaded him to give it another try.

The next night, they waited until the family had retired to bed before stepping out of their hiding place. This time, just as they settled in to eat, the dog barked at them and rushed toward them. Frightened, Mr. Field Mouse ran and just barely evaded the dog. Out of breadth, he said to his friend, "Your life is full of danger. I don't think I can cope."

"Nonsense!" said Mr. House Rat. "You just have to be careful. If you lived here, you would know how to avoid all the obstacles in your way. I have shelter from the rain compared, and you do not, and I really do not have to work for my food. I have learned how to avoid danger. Give it another night."

The next night, the two animals waited until the dog had been let out of the house to do his business before they ventured into the dining room to eat. The food was delicious, and they were absorbed in eating as much as they could.

Suddenly, out of nowhere, the cat jumped onto the table and overturned a plate as he ran toward the intruders. He narrowly missed Mr. Field Mouse, who remained oblivious as he gnawed on a chicken leg.

"Quick!" said Mr. House Rat. "Get down and run as fast as you can to the hole!"

"Why?" said Mr. Field Mouse.

"The cat has seen us," Mr. House Rat hissed. "You must move quickly if you want your family to see you in the morning."

Both scampered away from the cat and entered the tunnel just in time.

"Oh my! Oh my!" said Mr. Field Mouse. "Your life is fraught with danger. I don't think I can live such a life. I prefer my quiet life in the forest. I know my home is not as beautiful as yours, but nobody is after me. The rich life is not for me. I am happy being poor."

Mr. Field Mouse said good-bye to Mr. House Rat and returned to his home in the forest.

About the Author

Elder Dr. Doris Oji, JP and Ada Ukwu of Aro, is from Arochukwu. She served as a principal of several government secondary schools in Imo and Abia States of Nigeria for thirty-four years and retired as director of schools. She is very active in women's affairs in Arochukwu and is blessed with children and grandchildren.

Printed in the United States
By Bookmasters